"Justin!" Mom screamed

She, Bill, and Rachel stood at the edge of the mud with panicked looks on their faces.

"I can't get out!" I yelled.

Mom turned to Bill. "Do something!"

I was still sinking. The mud was up to my waist now.

Bill ducked into the brush and came back with a long branch. I was just able to grab the thinnest twigs at the end of the branch, but when I tried to hold on, they broke off.

Meanwhile, the mud was just below my ribs. It was the weirdest sensation. I was being swallowed up by the deep, thick brown muck.

"Just hold on, hon." Mom stood at the edge of the mud with a terrified expression on her face. "Just hold on. We're going to help you."

It couldn't be happening to me. I couldn't be sinking in the mud. It had to be happening to someone else.

It was up to my armpits now. Only my head and my forearms were out of the mud. As I slowly slid lower, I kept imagining my feet hitting something firm that would stop my descent. But there was nothing . . .

AGAINST THE ODDS™: Shark Bite
AGAINST THE ODDS™: Grizzly Attack
AGAINST THE ODDS™: Buzzard's Feast
AGAINST THE ODDS™: Gator Prey

By Todd Strasser

From Minstrel Books
Published by Pocket Books

TODD STRASSER
AGAINST THE ODDS™

GATOR PREY

A MINSTREL® BOOK

Published by POCKET BOOKS
New York London Toronto Sydney Tokyo Singapore

A MINSTREL PAPERBACK *Original*

 A Minstrel Book published by
POCKET BOOKS, a division of Simon & Schuster Inc.
1230 Avenue of the Americas, New York, NY 10020

TM and Copyright © 1999 by Todd Strasser

ISBN: 0-671-02312-8

First Minstrel Books printing March 1999

10 9 8 7 6 5 4 3 2 1

A MINSTREL BOOK and colophon are registered trademarks of Simon & Schuster Inc.

Front cover illustration by Franco Accornero

Printed in the U.S.A.

To Eli and Emma Fuchsberg

1

"**S**orry, Mrs. Thomas, but the mechanic didn't come in this morning," said the man behind the airport counter.

"Is there something wrong with my plane?" my mother asked.

"I don't think so, ma'am," the man said. "There were just a few things in the electrical system he said he wanted to check out."

"But did he say anything was actually wrong?" Mom asked.

The man behind the counter shook his head. "I can't say, ma'am."

Mom turned to me.

"Is there a problem?" I asked.

"I don't know," Mom answered. "But I don't see how we can take a chance, Justin. We can't fly unless the plane checks out one hundred percent."

"Gee, that's too bad, Mom." If we couldn't fly, it meant we couldn't go on the trip to Key West Mom had planned with her boyfriend, Bill. I can't say I was disappointed.

Mom gave me a smirk. "Come on, Justin, you could at least *pretend* you're disappointed."

"You going to call Bill?" I asked.

Mom shook her head. "He's already on his way over. We'll have to tell him when he gets here."

Mom and I walked over to the tiny waiting room and sat down. We were in the Vero Beach municipal airport building. The municipal airport was where Mom kept her plane. The building was air-conditioned, so we chose to wait inside rather than out in the scalding Florida sun.

"Think Bill will be disappointed?" I asked.

Mom nodded silently. She and Bill had been dating for a couple of months. He was the first guy Mom had seen since Dad died almost three years ago. Bill was divorced and lived with his daughter.

As we sat in the waiting room, I quickly planned out how I would spend the day now that I wouldn't have to be with Bill. I can't say that I was a big fan of Bill's, but what really had me freaked about this trip was that Bill was bringing his daughter. All I knew about her was that she was fourteen, a year older than me.

Someone had left a newspaper folded up on one of the waiting-room seats. Mom picked it up and started to read. On the front page was a photo of a line of burning trees with huge flames and dark smoke billowing above them. Two firefighters were running away from the fire and toward the camera. You definitely got the feeling that the fire was out of control.

We were having one of the driest springs ever in Florida. Brush and forest fires had become a serious problem, burning through entire communities and leaving hundreds of families homeless.

Through the waiting-room window I saw Bill's car enter the parking lot. You couldn't miss his car. It was a big Mercedes with a shiny hood ornament of a mermaid where the three-spoked emblem usually stood. It was the kind of car that practically yelled out to everyone, "Hey! Look! The guy driving this car must be rich!"

The funny thing was that, as far as I knew, Bill wasn't even close to rich. He was a real estate agent, but he didn't sell mansions or even houses. Instead he mostly sold condos to old people who came down to Florida to enjoy their "sunset" years.

Bill steered the big car around to the front of the parking lot and (wouldn't you know it!) pulled into a handicapped-only space. I was pretty sure that neither Bill nor his daughter was handicapped. Except maybe in the head.

Bill got out wearing greenish reflecting wrap-around sunglasses. The kind of glasses guys who think they're awesome cool wear. He was an average-size guy with short black hair and you could see that he'd probably had a pretty good build once. But now his gut hung over his belt and he was kind of flabby.

I expected the passenger door to open and Bill's daughter to get out. But the door stayed closed.

Instead, Bill bent down and stuck his head back into the Benz. I couldn't see his face, but I had the feeling he was talking to someone inside. That made me smile.

"What's so funny?" Mom asked.

"Looks like I'm not the only one who doesn't want to go on this trip," I said.

"You don't know what they're talking about," Mom replied.

"I know that when someone wants to fly down to Key West they get out of the car," I said.

"You don't know why she hasn't gotten out of the car yet," Mom argued. "She could be looking for something, or fixing her hair."

"Sure, Mom. Whatever."

Mom leaned toward me and gave me her serious look. I knew a lecture was coming. Luckily for me, with Bill right outside it would have to be a short lecture.

"Seriously, Justin," Mom began, "I want you to give Bill and Rachel a chance. I don't know what's come over you lately, but you've become very intolerant."

"Meaning?"

"Meaning you take one look at someone and make up your mind instantly," Mom went on. "And you shouldn't. You can't always go by first impressions. You can't just judge someone by their appearance."

"I don't," I said.

"Yes, you do," Mom said. "You divide the world into groups. Mostly, I might add, jocks and everyone else."

"Well, that's true." I grinned. "You're either a jock or you're not."

"And what am I?" Mom asked.

"You're over the hill, Mom," I said with a wink.

Mom made a fist like she wanted to punch me, but she was smiling. Even when she was really ticked at me, I could always make her smile.

Outside Bill went around to the passenger side of the Benz. He had a big frown on his face, as if he was pretty annoyed. He opened the passenger door. I got a brief glance of someone inside before Bill stuck his head in and blocked my view.

"Still think she's fixing her hair?" I asked Mom.

"Don't be a smart aleck," Mom grumbled.

"Why don't you just go out and tell Bill the trip is off?" I suggested. "You might save him a lot of grief."

Mom sighed and nodded. She had just started to get up when Bill backed away from the passenger door of the Benz and pulled it open.

A girl got out. At least, I assumed it was a girl. She was wearing black clothes, and her hair was dyed bright red. The gold hoops piercing her ears and nose glistened in the sunlight. At my school we called kids who dressed like that punkers.

Inside the terminal waiting room, I turned to my mom. "Know what?"

"What?" Mom asked.

"It's a good thing we're not going. Because there is no way I would ever spend a weekend in Key West with her."

2

Bill and Little Miss Punker came toward the terminal. You could tell so much by the way they walked. Bill marched along with his chest—and belly—puffed out. Rachel trudged behind him with her head bowed like she was being led to jail.

"How come we don't just go out and tell them the trip's off?" I asked Mom.

"It's cooler in here," she answered.

I can't say her answer rested well with me, but by then it was too late. Bill and his daughter came through the automatic sliding doors and we all did the big face-to-face.

"Hey, Justin." Bill slid his sunglasses up on his head and offered me his hand. I shook it unenthusiastically.

"You must be Rachel," Mom said to Little Miss Punker.

Bill's daughter crossed her arms and nodded. She gave me a quick glance out of the corner of her eye. She definitely looked seriously less than happy.

"Great." Bill clapped his hands together. "I'm just going to go back out to the car and get the bags and—"

"I'm afraid we have a problem, Bill," Mom interrupted him. "The mechanic didn't finish checking out the plane."

"So?" Bill asked.

"I don't feel comfortable," Mom said.

Bill wrinkled his forehead. "How's that?"

"Something could be wrong," Mom answered.

"Wait a minute, Sara," Bill said. "You just said the mechanic didn't finish checking out the plane. Is it something you can check out yourself?"

"Well . . ." Mom hesitated for a moment. "I always do a check list before takeoff."

"Then what's the problem?" Bill asked.

"You wouldn't want something to malfunction," Mom said.

"Like what?" asked Bill.

"It could be anything," Mom replied. "The autopilot, for instance."

"I thought you flew the plane, Sara," Bill said. "Not some machine."

"Well, I do," Mom said. "The autopilot is a backup system. In case of an emergency."

"What kind of emergency?" Bill asked.

"Bad weather," Mom said.

Bill rubbed his chin. "Sixty odd years ago Lindbergh flew across the Atlantic in fog. He didn't have autopilot. You're telling me that on a clear, sunny morning like this we can't hop down to Key West? How'd they fly all those years before autopilot was invented?"

"By visual navigation and compass," Mom answered. "But that's not the point—"

"Of course it's the point," Bill cut her short. "We can be down there in two hours, Sara. We're not flying at night or in bad weather. You just go south until you see the Keys and then follow them. It couldn't be easier."

Mom bit her lip. I could see that she was wavering. That was bad. Wavering meant we might have to spend the weekend with Bill and Little Miss Punker after all.

"That's not the point," I said. "Mom just used the autopilot as an example of what might go wrong. It could be something else."

"Sure, it could be anything," Bill replied. "And the mechanic could've checked the whole plane out and something might still be wrong. But if you want to look at it that way, no one should ever fly."

I started to open my mouth, but he saw it and started in again.

"I mean, where's your sense of adventure?" he asked. "People traveled the globe for thousands of years before they even had maps, much less electronics. I've got a nonrefundable deposit on two rooms at the Palm Resort with great ocean views. Couple of hours from now we'll be out on the deck sipping piña coladas."

"Me, too?" I asked archly since piña coladas had rum in them and I was way underage.

"No, not you," Mom said. She turned to Bill. "I don't know. I mean, I think in some ways you're right. But I've never flown unless everything was perfect. It makes me nervous."

"And I'm telling you there's nothing to be nervous about," Bill replied. "No one's said anything wasn't perfect. And it's not like we're taking a long trip. It's not like there's bad weather. How long have you been flying, Sara?"

"All my life, practically," Mom answered.

"And that was because your dad had a plane and he taught you," Bill said. "Did he always have all these fancy electronics?"

"No, not in the beginning," Mom said.

"See?" Bill said.

All through this conversation Little Miss Punker Rachel stood off to one side with her arms crossed, not even looking at us. But I was pretty sure she was listening. Despite what my mom said, I knew her type. The trouble with kids like her was that they always thought they were so incredibly cool. So totally above it all. At our school the punkers were the natural enemies of the jocks.

"I don't think it's fair to ask Mom to fly if she's not comfortable," I argued. "After all, she's the pilot. Not only is it her plane, but she's the one who has to feel responsible for the rest of us."

Bill's face clouded over. "Sara, I'd like to talk to you in private for a moment."

He marched into a corner of the waiting room and my mom followed. I really hated that. You have to understand what my mom used to be like before Dad died. I mean, I know she's a mother and everything, but she was also fairly amazing. She didn't just fly her own plane. She had her own business, and ran marathons, and did all kinds of relatively extreme athletic stuff for a mother.

She still had the business, but she'd stopped running, and this was probably only the second time since Dad died that we'd been out to the airport. Dad's death had really shaken her, and her whole attitude had changed. She just seemed a lot less sure of herself.

Of course, Dad's death had affected me, too. I was sometimes a lot less sure of things. Other than the fact that I was definitely *sure* I didn't want to go to Key West.

Mom and Bill stood off in a corner and talked. I should say Bill talked, since he did all the grumbling and gesturing while she just stood there nodding. That was another thing about Dad. He used to talk to Mom. Not at her. From where I stood, it looked like Bill was talking at Mom the way a coach chews out a player who's been slacking off in practice. You could tell that he really didn't want to hear what she had to say. He just wanted her to hear what he had to say. He just wanted to have his way.

When Bill dragged Mom off, Punk Rachel found a seat and slumped down into it. She sat there staring at her black fingernails with a sour expression on her face that basically said this was the last place on earth she wanted to be. I was kind of surprised she wasn't plugged into a Discman or something. Maybe that was what she and Bill had argued about in the car.

Now she just sat there looking like she didn't care what happened.

Bill finished his talk with Mom. He came back toward us and she followed. One look at Mom's face and I knew she'd lost the argument. Like it or not, we were going to Key West.

3

A little while later, the four of us sat in the plane while Mom went down a checklist making sure all the systems were working. Mom's plane was a four-seater single-engine prop. It had two seats in front and two behind, pretty much like a compact car with wings and a tail. Mom sat in front with Bill while I sat in back next to the silent punkette.

So far Rachel hadn't said a word. But it was going to be interesting to see how long she could stay quiet. Like I said, Mom's plane was about as small as you could get and still squeeze four people inside. Rachel and I were practically shoulder to shoulder.

In front, Mom handled the controls. Next to her, Bill had an aeronautical chart on his lap.

Aeronautical charts are sort of like regular maps, only they emphasize the stuff you're most likely to see from the air, like highways and train tracks and lakes and mountains. And they leave out things like state lines. In this case, most of the chart showed Lake Okeechobee, the giant lake that sits almost in the center of southern Florida.

Everything checked out in the plane. We taxied out to the runway and had to wait for a moment while another plane came in for a landing.

"See, we're not the only ones flying today," Bill said in a teasing way. "Looks like other people are risking their lives, too."

The other plane landed and Mom swung our plane around to the foot of the runway. Up to that point, she really hadn't revved the engine. But now she pushed the throttle forward and the plane began to vibrate. If you've flown in a small plane, you know this is pretty normal. But if all you've flown in are jets, the shaking and rattling and loud engine noise of a small plane can be fairly freaky.

The plane lurched forward and started down the runway. As it picked up speed, I watched Rachel out of the corner of my eye. She grabbed the edge of her seat and squeezed so hard that her knuckles became white.

Now another possibility popped into my head. Maybe the argument in the car hadn't been about a Discman. And maybe her silence wasn't just punky obnoxiousness.

Maybe she was just really scared of small planes.

To get from Vero Beach to Key West, you fly over Lake Okeechobee. This isn't any ordinary lake. After the Great Lakes, it's one of the largest in the country. As we rose in the sky, I peered out the window to the north and saw tall plumes of grayish white smoke rising miles into the air. Those must have been some of the fires that they'd written about in the newspaper.

Since we were setting a course visually, Mom kept the plane at a lower altitude than she might have normally flown. This meant that pretty soon all we could see beneath us were the waters of Lake Okeechobee fanning out in every direction.

Bill still had the aeronautical chart spread out in his lap. I had to wonder what he was using as ground reference since everything under us was water.

With Rachel being tight-lipped and staring out the window, there wasn't much for me to do except let my thoughts drift. This whole trip was totally weird to me. Mom and me and Bill and Rachel going to Key West together . . .

Like it was some kind of tryout for something bigger.

Maybe marriage or something.

Which would mean a brand-new family combination plate.

Maybe Mom thought she was ready for it. But as far as having Bill for a stepdad and Little Miss Punker Rachel for a stepsister . . . this was definitely something I had totally no interest in.

And it wasn't because I had something against punkers. If they wanted to dye their hair and pierce themselves, that was their business. The trouble was that they were always ready to fight. Like they were paranoid. If you weren't one of them, you were automatically the enemy. And the last thing I wanted to do in life was spend the next few years in the same house with someone who treated me like an idiot just because I liked sports better than stoned-out bands with names like the Molten Phlegmwadz.

It was just about then that I noticed the shoreline of Lake Okeechobee off to our right.

Wait a minute . . .

Sensing that something might be wrong, I unhooked my seat belt and leaned forward to look over Bill's shoulder.

"Hon, what are you doing?" Mom asked.

17

"Looking at the chart," I answered.

"You shouldn't take your seat belt off," she said.

"I'll just be a second," I said.

But it took a lot longer than a second. I just couldn't find any recognizable landmarks on the chart or the ground. As far as I could tell, if we were heading south, the nearest shore should have been on our left, not our right.

I peered up toward the sun, but it was directly overhead, and no help in figuring out our direction.

"Something wrong?" Bill asked.

"Well, I'm not totally sure, but I think maybe we're headed in the wrong direction," I said.

Mom instantly frowned and glanced at Bill.

"That's ridiculous," Bill sputtered. "We're following the chart. And your mom has the autopilot running."

Mom glanced back at me and nodded. "He's right, hon."

I sat back in my seat and buckled my belt again. I might not have trusted Bill's chart-reading skills, but it was hard to argue with Mom and the autopilot.

4

It wasn't long before we were flying over ground again. Bill kept looking out the window, then trying to find our location on the aeronautical chart. You would have thought that a recognizable landmark would pop up sooner or later, but Bill kept looking back and forth from chart to window as if he couldn't get a fix on things.

"Ahem." About ten minutes later he cleared his throat. "I hate to say it, but I can't figure out where we are."

Mom gave him a worried look. "We should be just south of the lake."

"I know," Bill said. "But I haven't seen anything that matches up with the chart."

For the last few minutes, I had been checking the dials in the instrument panel. The problem was, with Bill sitting in front of me, I couldn't see them all. Now I was seriously beginning to wonder. Once again I undid my seat belt and leaned forward.

"Now what?" Bill asked sharply. He sounded ticked off.

Instead of answering, I reached past him and pointed at the compass.

"Son of a gun!" Bill said in an astonished tone.

"We're going in the exact opposite direction of the way we should be going," I said.

Mom's reaction was instantaneous. She quickly began studying the rest of the dials in the panel. Then she banked the plane around in a wide circle. "My fault. I set the autopilot and Loran coordinates wrong. I guess I'm a little rusty."

Bill shifted the chart in his lap and started to recheck our location. "Okay, now I see where we are. We're a bit northwest of Okeechobee. It's okay, Sara. It's been a while since you've been in the pilot's seat. All we have to do is head south."

Mom adjusted the autopilot and Loran coordinates. Now the broad, shimmering waters of Lake Okeechobee were on our left.

"That wasn't so bad," Bill said. "We had to travel west anyway to get to the Keys. We did go north a bit, but I bet no more than fifty miles out of our way."

"It's a hundred miles when you figure in the backtracking," I corrected him.

Bill turned and glowered at me for a moment.

"Maybe we ought to go back to Vero Beach," Mom said nervously.

"Oh, come on, Sara. We're fine now." Bill gestured at the compass. "We're headed in the right direction. You don't throw in the towel just because of one little mistake. I guarantee you, nothing else is going to go wrong. Trust me."

Famous last words.

5

We were headed south now. It was probably around 1 P.M. and the sun was still pretty much right above us. Lake Okeechobee had just about disappeared in the distance behind us. Below was the vast river of grass known as the Everglades.

"I think it might be a good idea to stop and refuel," Mom said.

Bill pointed at the fuel gauges. "Why? We've still got a little over half in each tank."

Mom's plane had two fuel tanks. One in each wing.

"I just want to be sure," Mom said.

"Come on, Sara," Bill said impatiently. "That's probably enough gas to get us down to Key West and back twice!"

"You don't want to take chances, Bill," Mom replied. "The kids, remember?"

Bill sighed and gave in. "Okay, so let's refuel."

"Look on the map for an airport between here and Key West," Mom said. "The key will tell you if they pump fuel to the public."

Bill ran his finger down the map. "Here we go. Jerome."

"How far?" Mom asked.

"Fifty miles, maybe."

"Good. We'll stop there."

For the next forty minutes we enjoyed a smooth flight. Rachel the Punker still hadn't uttered a word. She'd hardly moved either. She just stared out the window. Below us was either a lot to see or very little. It depended on your point of view. If mile after mile of swamp and marsh filled with tall brown clumps of saw grass, water, and huge flocks of birds didn't interest you, then it would have been a pretty boring flight.

"We should be getting close to Jerome," Mom said after a while. "See anything?"

We all peered out of our windows. Below us it was still mostly marsh and swamp, but here and there was an island with trees—what the locals called a hammock.

"There's something," Rachel suddenly said.

I have to admit that it was sort of shocking to hear her voice after so long a silence. Since what she was looking at was over on her side of the plane, I couldn't see it.

"Where?" Bill pressed his forehead against his window.

"Look straight out," Rachel said. "Almost to the horizon. You'll see that long orange thing."

"A wind sock," Mom said.

Bill looked for a while. "Okay, now I see it. Wow, you've got some eyes, babe."

Babe? Was that what he called his daughter?

Mom banked the plane and started to descend. Another fifteen minutes passed. Then a small airfield came into view. And I mean, small. The field itself was grass. A shack stood beside it. Behind the shack half a dozen small planes were parked.

Mom got on the radio and tried to raise someone. "Jerome traffic. This is Cherokee eight-four-eleven Charlie downwind for the runway. Do you read?"

Except for some faint static, the radio was silent. Mom tried again. "Jerome traffic. This is Cherokee eight-four-eleven Charlie downwind for the runway. Requesting clearance to land."

Mom circled the airfield four times, repeatedly calling down, but no one answered.

"What do we do now?" Bill asked once it had become obvious that the airfield was unattended.

"Where's the next airfield?" Mom asked. Her voice sounded strained.

Bill checked the map. "Headed in the direction we want to go, about eighty miles."

"Eighty?" Mom said. "Where's that?"

"Marathon," Bill answered.

Mom shook her head. "No. I'm not taking this plane out over the Gulf when we're low on fuel. What's the closest airfield over land?"

"Homestead," Bill said.

"Good," Mom said. "I know that airstrip. And the Air Force base is nearby in case of an emergency."

Mom banked the plane toward the east. Suddenly the engine sputtered. The plane rattled.

"What was that?" Bill gasped.

The engine sputtered again.

"Fuel." Mom's answer was clipped. She was busy studying the instrument panel.

"It says it's almost a quarter full." Bill tapped the fuel gauge with his knuckle.

The engine was now sputtering continually. The prop was slowing. The nose of the plane tilted down and we started to lose altitude. Rachel gave me a frightened look. Mom reached up to the ceiling for the fuel selector valve that switched to the other wing tank.

Mom, Bill, and I were busy looking at the instrument panels. I just wanted to see the altimeter level out and stop dropping.

"Oh, my gosh!" Rachel suddenly gasped.

We all looked up.

Through the windshield we saw gray.

But it wasn't a cloud.

It was a huge flock of birds.

6

When pilots talk about what happened to us, they say we "ingested birds." In our case, I think there were three, but I'm not sure because by the time they reached me they were nothing but feathers and blood and guts.

The first one crashed through the windshield and smashed into Mom's face.

"Mom!" I shouted. The wind rushed in and feathers began to swirl around inside the cockpit. We were splattered with blood.

Bill reached over and tried to help. "Sara, are you okay?"

I'm not sure Mom was conscious. I'm pretty sure she didn't answer Bill. We probably couldn't have heard her even if she had. All you could hear was the roar of the wind and the sounds of things flapping and banging around in the cockpit. By now the other birds had been ingested and everything was total mayhem.

That was when the engine cut out altogether. The prop stopped spinning and sat there in front of us. An eerie quiet fell over the airplane. We could hear the whistle of the wind as we glided downward.

"Mom? *Mom!*" I reached forward and shook her shoulders. She felt limp and loose, like an old cloth doll. Then she raised her head and seemed to wake up a little. "Wha . . . ?"

"The motor stopped!" I shouted.

I think Mom was still half out of it. With a trembling hand she pressed the starter button. The starter motor whined. The prop jerked over slowly, as if it were struggling. The wind continued to whistle.

"What's going on?" Bill gasped.

Mom gave up on the starter button and gripped the wheel with both hands. "Hold on. We're going down."

7

The weird thing about crashing in a small airplane is that it happens much slower than when you're in a car. If you're wondering how I know, it's because I was in the car with Dad the night he died. In a car it's like *Screech! Bang! Boom!* It all happens in a couple of seconds. You see the truck coming around the curb toward you and by the time you realize that it's crossing the yellow lines, it's too late to get out of the way.

In the plane it must have been ten, twenty seconds. Maybe even half a minute. Compared to the car it was an eternity.

No one said a word. But we all had plenty of time to think. I thought about Dad and me in that crash, and now Mom and me in the plane. It was like, there goes the family!

Sure, I was scared out of my brains. But it wasn't a hopeless scared. It was a hopeful scared. It was, Just hold on! We can make it!

Maybe that was why no one talked, or screamed.

The ground was coming up fast. Only it wasn't ground. It was sparkling sunlit water and clumps of brown and green saw grass. Mom was angling the plane away from any hammocks where the trees were. As you can probably imagine, trees and airplanes are a really, really bad combination.

Just before we hit, she pulled back hard on the wheel to try to level the plane out, and dropped the flaps to slow us down. A sound somewhere between a crinkle and a hiss followed as we cut through the tops of a couple of clumps of saw grass.

Then we hit—hard.

8

The next thing I remember, the plane was nose down, the tail sticking up out of the water. I was hanging facedown in my seat. The only things that prevented me from falling forward into Mom's seat were my seat belt and shoulder straps.

It was dark inside the plane. Not pitch black like night. More like we were in a deep shadow. You could hear hissing where the water was seeping into the engine compartment and touching the still hot parts of the engine. You could also hear water dribbling into the cabin. It sounded like a dozen fast-running faucet leaks. I turned my head and looked out. Water was rippling against the lower half of my window. That meant the front half of the plane was partly submerged.

"Mom?" I said.

She didn't answer. An oozing brown clump of grass, mud, and roots now filled the space where the windshield used to be.

"Bill?" I said.

"Huh?" He was awake, but sounded dazed.

I turned and looked at Rachel and found her staring back at me. A thin stream of red blood trickled out of a cut on the bridge of her nose.

"You okay?" I asked.

Instead of answering, she touched her nose, then stared down at the blood smeared on her fingertips.

"We gotta get out of here," Bill gasped in the front and started to undo his seat belt and shoulder harness.

"We have to help my mom," I said, struggling to undo my own belt and harness. It wasn't east to open the clasps when you were hanging with all your weight against them.

Bill managed to undo his belt and straps. He reached for the door handle and put his shoulder to the door. He got it open maybe half an inch, then murky brown water began to pour in.

"Close it!" I yelled, scared that the cockpit would flood before we could get out.

Bill twisted around and stared at me with

wide, frightened eyes. "How're we gonna get out?"

Good question, I thought. If we couldn't open the doors, what other choices did we have? The broken windshield? But that was filled with grass, roots, and mud. We were lucky that junk was keeping the water out or we might all have drowned by now. Then I remembered that the plane had a small baggage door about halfway up the tail. We used it to stow stuff in the back. I'd never seen it opened from the inside, but if we were lucky there'd be a way to do it.

"I'm gonna try something," I yelled. "In the meantime, try to get my mom out of her seat."

Bracing myself against the inside of the cabin, I tried to climb between my seat and Rachel's. I had to undo the cargo straps, and as soon as I did, a suitcase and a couple of overnight bags tumbled forward and blocked my path. Each time I tried to push them out of the way, they'd just fall back into the space between the two seats and block me again.

"Here, give them to me," Rachel said.

Good idea, I thought. Instead of trying to push them away, I pulled them down one by one until I was able to climb up into the tail of the plane.

It was dark up there and I had to feel around. I finally found the baggage door, but I couldn't find an inside latch or knob. Finally I just scrunched up and pushed hard against it with my feet. Suddenly it gave and fell into the water outside with a splash.

Bright sunlight streamed in, making me squint. From my perch in the plane's tail, I looked back down into the cabin and found Bill and Rachel staring up at me.

"Where's my mom?" I asked, alarmed.

Bill blinked with astonishment. Had he just forgotten about her? The level of the water at the front of the cockpit was rising and my mom was hanging there face down by her harness. For all I knew, she might already have been underwater!

Bill bent down and started to fumble with Mom's seat belt and harness, but I didn't trust him.

"Climb past me and get out," I said to Rachel. I figured it would be easier for me to get back into the cabin if she wasn't in the way.

She frowned. "Aren't you getting out?"

"I have to make sure my mom's okay," I answered, and helped her climb up past me and wriggle out of the baggage door.

Splash! Rachel dropped down into the marsh water outside the plane. Meanwhile I lowered myself through the seats and back into the cockpit where Bill was still fumbling with Mom's belts.

"Mom?" I called.

"Hon?" She lifted her head with a groan. "My ankle."

"We're going to help you," I said.

Working together, Bill and I managed to undo her seat belt and shoulder harness. By now the water in the cockpit was nearly waist deep and just about the same level as outside.

"Ow! Stop!" Mom cried out when we tried to move her out of the pilot's seat. Bill and I hesitated.

"Where does it hut?" I asked.

Mom grimaced. "My ankle."

Moving more gingerly, we managed to help her out of the seat and up toward the plane's tail. It was clear that she couldn't put any weight on her ankle. Soon Bill and I were squeezed into the tail area. Sunlight streamed in through the open hatch above us.

"Now what?" Bill asked grimly.

I looked up at the baggage door and wondered how in the world we could get Mom up there and out of the plane.

Suddenly a shadow appeared in the doorway. Rachel stuck her head in. "How's it going?" she asked.

"How'd you get up there?" I asked, astonished.

"I climbed back up on the outside," she answered. "So what's the story?"

"My mom's hurt her ankle," I answered. "I don't know how bad it is, but I doubt she'll be able to climb up to the tail to get out."

Rachel stared down at us for a moment and then said, "Maybe she won't have to."

I found myself listening in amazement as Little Miss Punker explained her plan. "The three of us have to climb up as high as we can on the tail of the plane," she said. "Right now most of the weight is in the front. But depending on how far up the fulcrum is, we may be able to leverage the plane to horizontal."

Fulcrum? Leverage?

She sounded like an engineer.

"Then what?" I asked.

Rachel scowled at me as if the answer was incredibly obvious. "Then we get your mom out."

9

Bill climbed up and sat half in and half out of the baggage door. Then I started to climb up into the tail. Even before I'd got all the way up, I could feel the tail of the plane start to drop. It was like being on the high end of an unusually steep and slow seesaw. Very gradually the tail started to come down. Below me in the plane's cabin, Mom held on to a seat as the plane slowly became horizontal.

Soon the nose of the plane and the prop came out of the water, covered with brownish muck and green water weeds. Meanwhile the tail now lay level with the water.

Rachel told her dad to climb all the way out of the door, but keep his weight on the tail to make sure the plane didn't tip up again. I crouched in the tail and peered out at Rachel, who stood chest deep in the marshy water.

"Should I try to bring Mom out this way?" I asked.

Rachel gave me a funny look. "No. Now we can open the doors and take her out."

She was right, of course. I just hadn't thought of it. Now that the plane was level in the water, we could open the doors. It wouldn't matter if a little more water floated in. I crawled out of the baggage door and into the cool marsh water. While Bill held on to the tail, Rachel and I waded to the door of the plane. The water came up to our chests and the bottom was soft and muddy. We managed to pull the door open. Inside, Mom was leaning against my old seat. She was grimacing in pain, but a small, crooked smile crossed her lips.

"That was an excellent idea, Rachel," she said.

"Thanks," replied Bill's daughter.

"Now let's get you out," I said, reaching in toward my mom.

"Wait," Rachel said. "We have to figure out what we're going to do with her first."

Again she was right. With Mom's bad ankle, it wouldn't be easy for her to make her way through the chest-deep water of the marsh.

"Life preservers," I said.

"Under the seats," said Mom.

It wasn't long before we'd dug the four life preservers out from under the seats and inflated them. We lashed them together with cargo belts and bungee cords. The result was a small raft that Mom could float on while we pulled her through the marsh to safety.

Not that I knew where safety was. But it definitely wasn't in this plane in the middle of the marsh.

Once we got Mom out of the plane and onto the raft, we started to look around, hoping to figure out where to go. Not that you can see a lot when you're chest deep in water and surrounded on all sides by clumps of tall brown and green saw grass. I knew about saw grass from school. From a distance it sort of looked like a big clump of reeds, but up close you could see the sharp, saw-toothed edges that could cut right through skin.

"See anything?" Rachel asked me while she held on to Mom's raft to keep her from drifting away.

"Nothing," I answered. It was weird how we were suddenly speaking to each other as if we'd known each other for years. "Wait, I've got an idea."

I grabbed one of the plane's wings and hauled myself up out of the water. Then I climbed on top of the cabin. Now I could see over the saw grass.

"Based on the tops of the trees in the distance," I called back down, "it looks like there's a hammock about half a mile away."

"Good," Rachel called back from down in the water. "Before we go, we should see if there's anything else in the cabin we can use."

Another good suggestion. I sat down on top of the cabin, then slid off it and crawled inside to look for emergency supplies.

"What's the plan?" Bill asked as he waded toward us. It was sort of weird to hear him ask. I was used to hearing him make the decisions and give the orders.

Rachel explained that we had to take some supplies and head for the hammock to get out of the water.

Her father's face turned pale. "What about the alligators?"

10

Alligators . . . Like actors in a horror movie we all started to look around, nervously searching for the unseen monsters. Here we were, chest deep in water and a long way from the nearest dry land. We'd been so focused on trying to survive our problems in the air that it hadn't occurred to us to think about the ones we might have on the ground. Or, in this case, in the water.

"The Everglades are full of them," Bill said.

"Then I think we'd better head for that hammock now," I said. "The sooner we're out of the water the better."

"I have news for you," Bill said. "Gators can get out of the water, too. And you'd be amazed at how fast they can travel on land."

"Just don't tell me they can climb trees," I said and started to pull Mom on her life preserver raft through the murky water.

But Bill wasn't finished with his book report on alligators. "One thing I heard once was, if one does come after you on land, don't run straight. Try to zigzag. Gators can run pretty fast, but they have a lot of trouble changing direction."

We weren't on land. We were in the water.

"What if one comes after you in the water?" I asked.

"Hold your breath," Bill replied grimly.

"No, I know what you do," Rachel said to her father as we waded around the tall clumps of saw grass, pulling Mom. "Remember that time we saw the guy wrestle one?"

"But he was a professional," Bill said.

"He said alligator jaws are really powerful when it comes to closing on things, but really weak when it comes to opening," Rachel said. "He said you have to try to get your arm around their mouth and keep it closed."

"Oh, sure." Bill chuckled nervously. "I'd like to see you try that with a twelve-footer."

As we wound our way around the clumps of saw grass, we saw that Bill was right. The Everglades were full of alligators. But, luckily, none were twelve-footers. With their bumpy nostrils and eyes and scaly bodies, they looked like they belonged in prehistoric dinosaur times. The ones we saw at first were smallish by alligator standards—maybe four or five feet long. They were floating among the lily pads or sunning themselves on the edges of the saw grass clumps. Some hardly seemed to notice us. Others dropped out of sight beneath the water's surface like reptilian submarines.

We moved slowly and nervously through the marsh waters. The bottom, when we could feel it, was either oozy muck or a tangle of roots that snagged on our pants and tripped up our feet. Above us, the sun burned down on the tops of our heads. It was a weird sensation. From the chest down, we were cooled by the waters. From the chest up we were scalded by the sun.

Hardly a second passed that I didn't imagine some huge alligator swimming up behind me and clamping its jaws around one of my legs.

"Ow!" Bill yelped after trying to pull himself forward by grabbing at a clump of saw grass. He yanked his hand away and stared down at his palm. The deep scratches left thin trails of blood.

"This stuff is dangerous," he moaned.

"That's why they call it saw grass," Rachel said.

We kept plodding, struggling, half-swimming, half-wading slowly toward the small island of trees in the distance. Every now and then a white egret or bluish gray heron would take flight ahead of us, slowly flapping its broad wings and lifting its long body into the air. Scary-looking greenish blue dragonflies with big round eyes and long tails darted past and hovered above us. At one point a whole bunch of small brown birds lifted off like a cloud flying this way and that until disappearing in the distance.

The raft of life preservers helped Mom stay afloat, but didn't keep her out of the water. She held on to them, her face lined with pain.

"How's the ankle, Mom?" I asked.

"Hurts like the dickens," she groaned.

"Think you sprained it?" I asked.

"It's worse than that," she answered.

"Jeez!" In the water ahead of us Bill suddenly stopped and pointed. A dozen feet away, something was making a wiggling wake just below the surface.

"Alligator?" I asked.

"Snake," Bill replied. "Probably a water moccasin. They're poisonous. The Everglades are full of rattlers, too."

The snake in the water vanished behind a clump of saw grass. We started moving again.

I was beginning to think that Bill was full of all kinds of information I didn't want to hear.

It took a long time to reach the island. The sun burned the tops of our heads and the backs of our necks. Fighting through the water, muck, and roots was exhausting. Especially since we all had our clothes and shoes on.

By the time we crawled through the reeds at the edge of the hammock and helped ease Mom out of the water, we were so tired we all dropped to the ground in a state of exhaustion. I swam the 1,500- and 3,000-meter events on the school swim team, but it was hard to recall if I'd ever felt that tired before.

I don't know how long I lay there on the dry ground. The dominant sensation I felt was total fatigue. But there were other sensations—the hot sun pressing down, for instance. And, on various parts of my body, I also felt slight stinging sensations, but these I figured were just scrapes and small cuts I'd gotten while struggling through the saw grass marsh.

As I focused on what was around me, I saw the strangest looking bird I'd ever seen standing up in the brush about fifteen feet away. It had yellow legs and toes that were almost as long as the legs themselves. It had greenish wings and a blue body. Its head was also blue, except for a big white spot on its forehead. Its long beak was red, except for the tip, which was yellow.

It looked more like something a kid would draw in art class than a living creature. And the funny thing was the way it looked at me with one eye and then the other. As if I was the strange-looking one.

Who knows, maybe in the Everglades I was.

Meanwhile, I was growing increasingly uncomfortable because of the stinging spots on my body. It was just starting to dawn on me that something was biting me when I noticed Rachel staring at my arm. I looked down. Stuck on my arm was a fat dark greenish thing maybe three inches long. It looked like some kind of slug, only it stung where it was attached to my skin. In a reflex motion I tried to pick it off my arm. It slid through my fingers and stayed attached.

"Leech!" Rachel gasped.

11

Rachel, Bill, and I quickly yanked up our soggy pant legs. We each had half a dozen leeches on each calf and shin. Even though the pain wasn't great, it was a horrible feeling, knowing these disgusting creatures were sucking your blood and you couldn't get them off.

"What do we do?" Bill gasped.

"You're supposed to burn them off," Rachel said.

"Anyone got a dry match?" Bill asked.

"Check the stuff we brought from the plane," I said.

Lucky for us, Rachel found a waterproof container of matches. She struck one and turned toward me. "Hold your leg steady."

To get the leech off, Rachel had to hold the

match flame right under it, which meant keeping it pretty close to my skin. Hold your hand over a candle flame for an instant too long and you'll know how it felt. But there was no other way to get the leeches to let go.

"Ow!" Rachel let go of the match and pressed her fingertips to her lips. In the process of burning leeches, she'd held the match too long and it burned her fingers. She tossed the smoking stub of the match away.

"Careful," I warned her. "You don't want to start a fire."

The ground around us was as dry as tinder.

"Good point," Rachel answered and lit another match.

It took a while for us to burn the leeches off one another and take care of a few that had attached themselves to Mom.

"Got 'em all?" I asked, then shared a nervous look with Rachel and Bill. I think we all had the same idea at the same time: What if there were more in our wet clothes?

The only way to find out would be to pull off our clothes. Rachel must have realized that because she jumped up and hurried away through the brush along the shoreline. I took off in the other direction.

Once I was sure the others couldn't see me, I stripped off my wet clothes and turned them inside out. Sure enough, a couple of leeches were inside. Then, instead of putting the clothes back on, I laid them out in the sun to dry.

Exposed to the broiling-hot sun, my clothes dried pretty quickly. In the meantime, I inspected the small red wounds on my legs. For a moment I was worried that they might become infected. Then I remembered reading somewhere that doctors actually used to use leeches to treat patients. If we were lucky, we'd be okay.

After a while I pulled my clothes back on. They were still damp in spots, and where they were dry they were stiff from the mud and guck of the marsh. Believe me, it's that kind of experience that makes you appreciate clean clothes.

I headed back through the brush and reeds to the spot where I'd left Mom and the others. When I got back, Bill was there, but Rachel still hadn't returned. Mom was sitting with her back against a tree trunk. She looked pale and kept wincing in pain. Her left knee was bent, but her right leg lay straight out. When I looked down at her right foot, I felt a jolt. It was bent out at an odd angle. I wasn't much of a medical expert, but it was pretty obvious that she had a broken ankle.

"How's it feel?" I asked.

Mom shook her head. I knew it must have been bad because she wasn't the type who complained. This was a woman who once ran a marathon, came home, took a nap, then got up and cooked dinner.

For the first time since we'd gotten to the hammock, I looked around. It was nothing more than a raised piece of dry ground covered with trees and brush. Grayish green Spanish moss drooped from the tree branches, and birds flitted here and there. It felt wild and remote. You got the feeling that we were a long way from anything that you could begin to describe as civilization.

Rachel came back through the brush. Her hair was matted down. She looked tired, but in a way she looked better, too. She put her hands on her hips and looked around.

"Now what?" She asked the question we were all thinking.

"Guess we have to find our way out of here," Bill answered.

"What about Mom?" I asked.

"Does anyone know how to make a splint?" my mom asked.

Bill, Rachel, and I glanced at one another mutely.

"We'll need to find some straight branches or

flat pieces of wood," Mom said. "And something to tie them together."

"Maybe we could find some tree branches that end in a Y," I said. "We could turn them into crutches."

"Good idea," said Mom.

I turned and was about to head into the woods when Rachel stopped me.

"Wait," she said. "The one thing you don't want to do is get lost."

I hesitated. She was right.

"Break a small branch or twig every ten feet," Rachel suggested. "then you'll be able to find your way back."

I stared at her for a moment. "Did you learn that in the Girl Scouts or something?"

Rachel smirked. "Do I look like a Girl Scout to you?"

"Well, no," I admitted awkwardly. "It's just that . . . I don't know."

Rachel smiled a little and didn't say anything more.

12

We agreed to meet back there in an hour. I headed into the woods, leaving a trail of broken twigs and branches. The trees were covered with Spanish moss and vines, and filled with birds. A loud *rat-tat-tat* sound caught my attention. It must have been a woodpecker. I struggled through the thick brush, wishing I had a machete. Even in the shade of the trees it was oven hot and I was quickly covered with a slick film of sweat.

The first thing I realized was that this hammock was a lot bigger than I'd thought. Maybe it was even part of the mainland, but if it was, why weren't there any trails or other signs of humans?

I had a feeling it wouldn't be hard to find

the smaller pieces of wood for Mom's splint. What would be hard were the larger branches that she might be able to use as crutches. It wasn't easy to break branches off trees with my bare hands, especially branches that would be strong enough to use as crutches. But the trees were so dry that I soon figured out that I could climb up in them and then stomp on a limb until it cracked.

By the time I'd managed to break down two good branches, it was time to head back. I was glad Rachel had suggested breaking twigs because otherwise I never would have found my way.

When I got back, Rachel was already there. She'd found some straight sticks that were about an inch thick. Now she was using a rock to chip off the unnecessary twigs.

I showed her the thick Y-shaped branches I hoped we could turn into crutches.

"I figure we can use some of our clothes to pad the armpits," I said.

Rachel looked up at me. "Learn that in Boy Scouts?"

I shook my head. I didn't want to admit that I'd been a Boy Scout for two years, especially since I could hardly remember anything practical, except maybe how to tie a couple of knots.

Bill came out of the trees carrying several

thin, flat boards with chips of old, white paint flaking off them.

"Where'd you get those?" I asked, excited.

"I found an old rowboat," Bill answered.

Rachel immediately lifted her head. "A boat?"

"Don't get your hopes up," her father warned. "It was falling apart. The bottom was completely rotted out."

Rachel's shoulders sagged with disappointment.

"Hey, it still means that someone's been here," I said. "If they came by rowboat, we can't be that far from civilization, can we?"

"Hard to say," was Bill's reply.

I had to put those thoughts out of my mind and concentrate on the job at hand. Without tools, it took a while to turn the branches I'd found into crutches. But the worst part was making the splint for Mom's ankle. We broke down the boards from the rowboat, and then tore our extra shirts into long, thin strips.

But splinting Mom's ankle was horrible. The slightest touch caused her to cry out in pain. I couldn't stand it and went off into the woods and covered my ears. Bill and Rachel stayed and helped tie the boards tightly around Mom's ankle.

When the cries stopped, I went back. Mom was leaning against the tree. From the knee down her right leg was braced by two white boards tied tightly with the rags. Mom's face was pale and beaded with sweat and she looked exhausted by the ordeal. Bill looked pale, too, and Rachel was wiping tears from her own eyes. It wasn't pain, just the agony of watching someone else suffer.

By now the sun had started to angle into the western sky. For the first time I began to realize what it meant. We were about to spend a night in the Everglades.

13

In some ways we were very lucky. Except for Mom's broken ankle, we'd all come through the crash okay. And one of the emergency items I'd found in the plane was a water-purifying pump. The way it worked was pretty simple. You pumped by hand and forced the water through all kinds of filters that got rid of the stuff you didn't want to drink.

It was slow work and took about twenty minutes just to get a quart. But after an hour we had enough water. For food we had candy bars and trail mix. Not a lot, but enough to get through the night.

As the sun started to tilt lower in the west, the light grew less harsh and we were bombarded by vast swarms of mosquitoes. They hovered around us in clouds so thick it was hard to see through them. Even the hum they made was amazingly loud. Like you were in some kind of factory with machinery. There was no way to keep them away. We lay on the ground and tucked ourselves into balls. We tried burying our faces in our hands. I even tried rolling around. No matter how we tried to protect ourselves, they always found some bare skin, or just bit us right through our clothes.

Mom was in particularly bad shape because she couldn't really move. "I can't take this," she groaned as she covered her face with her hands. The backs of her hands were dark with hungry mosquitoes.

I wanted to help her, but I didn't know how. In desperation, I looked to Rachel. She might not have been a Girl Scout, but she'd come up with a lot of good ideas since the crash.

"Mud," she said.

Again, it sounded right.

I crawled toward Mom. "Lie down on your side."

Mom usually wasn't the kind of person who obeyed orders without questioning them. The fact that she did this time just showed how miserable she must have been.

With mosquitoes buzzing in our ears and biting into every exposed inch of our skin, Rachel and I crawled to a nearby mud hole and started to dig up handfuls of thick, claylike mud. Then we crawled back to Mom and began to cake her bare skin with mud.

Even Bill pitched in, grunting, "I almost feel like a kid playing with mud."

"I always wondered what a mud bath felt like," Mom said in an amazing show of humor, given the pain she must have been in.

By the time we finished Mom, she looked like some kind of monster in a cheap fifties monster flick. We'd caked her face, ears, and neck with mud. We'd covered her hands and every other inch of bare skin.

Next we did Bill, and then we did the same with ourselves.

"Know what's amazing?" I asked as I smeared myself with mud.

"I know what you're going to say. 'It feels great,'" Rachel said, as if she could read my mind.

It may sound hard to believe, but it really did feel good. It not only cut way down on the number of bites I was getting, but seemed to soothe the ones I already had.

It grew dark, and while we were all pretty tired, no one fell asleep. We just lay on the ground, trying not to move because moving made the mud crack and fall off. Fireflies with tiny blinking lights in their bodies floated in the air above us. An amazing chorus of chirps and calls filled our ears. Frogs and crickets, I guessed.

There were hoots of owls and grunts of animals we couldn't identify. The minutes passed slowly.

"Mom?" I asked. "How are you feeling?"

"If I don't move, it's not too bad," she answered.

"What do you think happened?" Rachel asked.

I knew she was referring to the plane crash.

"The left tank went dry and for some reason when I switched to the other tank nothing happened," Mom answered.

"It's my fault," Bill suddenly said.

I have to admit that I was surprised to hear him say that. And while I wasn't the kind of person who went around blaming people, in this case I knew he was right. Still, it was pretty amazing.

"I mean," he went on, "if I hadn't made us go on this trip this wouldn't have happened."

"No, it's my fault," Mom countered. "I should have had the sense to say no. The plane wasn't completely checked out. Maybe if I'd used it yesterday that wouldn't have mattered. But it's been a few months."

I didn't say anything, but inside I totally disagreed with her. I'd been there. I'd seen how

Bill had influenced her decision. It was almost like a peer-pressure thing. The kind of thing they lecture you in school about. Like, "Don't give in to peer pressure when you know it's wrong."

The way they talk to you about it, you pretty much assume it's a teenage thing like zits and popularity. It's kind of weird to think that adults deal with it, too. As if it's something you never grow out of.

"I don't think talking about whose fault it is is going to do anyone any good," Rachel suddenly said in the dark. "I think we should just be glad we're mostly okay and try to rest up for tomorrow."

Once again the best suggestion seemed to come from Rachel. In the dark, where I couldn't see her and could only hear her, it was weird. Based on the stuff she said, I would have expected a completely different kind of person. Definitely not a punker.

Even stranger was that I felt like I wanted to talk to her. If only to try to solve the mystery of why she looked so different from how she sounded. But with our parents around, there was no way I would ever say a word.

14

I can't say any of us got much sleep that night. You'd doze for a while, then wake to the sound of mosquitoes buzzing in your ear, or to feel a particularly annoying bite in a sensitive place. Then you'd sort of roll around on the ground and smear more mud on and try to go back to sleep.

We were up with the first light. You never saw a more sorry-looking bunch of people—covered with streaks and patches of dried mud, itchy, hungry, miserable. A few mosquitoes still hovered around and bit us now and then, but we were so tired and swollen that we ignored them.

"Now what?" I asked as I stood up and brushed some of the mud off.

"We have to get out of here," Bill said.

Nobody argued with that, so we helped Mom to her feet. I guess I should say we helped her up to her *foot,* since she had to keep the bad one off the ground. She winced and grimaced, but once we got her up and helped her onto the homemade crutches, she seemed to think she'd be okay.

"Which way?" I asked.

"Maybe we should head back to that rowboat Dad found," Rachel said.

"Believe me, babe," Bill said, "it'll never float."

"It's not that," said Rachel. "If someone left a boat there, they must have been going somewhere on land. Or maybe they came from somewhere. Maybe we'll find a trail."

It sounded like a reasonable idea. I was starting to think that it was really lucky that we had Rachel with us. We started into the woods, following the broken twigs and branches that Bill had used the evening before to find his way back. Luckily for us as soon as we got away from the shore, the ground became hard and dry and Mom was able to use the homemade crutches without worrying about the ends sinking into the ground.

"It's just about the end of the dry season," Rachel reminded us. "It's bad for the people with homes around those fires, but we're lucky it's so dry or we'd be sinking in mud."

Still, it was slow going. Mom had to stop and rest often and even with her foot in the splint you could see that she was in a lot of pain.

We finally reached the rowboat. It was pulled up on the shore in a small clearing. Bill was right. The bottom was rotted out. You couldn't use it for anything except wood.

"Someone left this boat here and went somewhere," Rachel surmised, looking around. "I have a feeling that wherever they went is where we want to go."

Again, you couldn't help but be amazed that someone who looked like her could think so clearly about everything.

"Justin and Rachel," Mom said, "why don't you two look around and see if there's a trail. In the meantime, I could use a little rest."

Rachel and I started through the undergrowth along the water's edge, looking for signs of a trail. For a while neither of us said anything. Twenty-four hours earlier I probably would have chalked it up to Rachel just being a punker. But now I had to wonder.

"Can I ask you something?" I said as we kicked our way through the underbrush.

"What?" Rachel asked. She was using a stick to beat away the prickly vines in our path.

63

"How come you know so much?" I said. "I mean, about what to do?"

"Who said I did?" she asked.

"Well, it's obvious," I said. "I mean, like that fulcrum stuff with the plane and covering up with mud to keep the mosquitoes off."

"I don't know." She shrugged. "Doesn't it just seem logical?"

"To you maybe," I said.

Rachel didn't say anything more, and I couldn't think of anything more to ask, so we just kept working our way through the brush.

"Here!" Rachel pointed into the woods. At first it was hard to see what she was pointing at. But then I saw it—a narrow path through the brush and trees.

I turned and cupped my hands around my mouth. "Mom! Bill! Can you hear me?"

"Yes." Bill's answer was faint and distant.

"We found something!" I yelled.

"Okay!" Bill yelled back. "We're coming!"

A little while later, following my voice, Bill came through the brush and Mom followed, hobbling on the crutches.

He frowned when he saw the "trail" we'd found.

"Doesn't look like anyone's used it in years," he grumbled.

"Still, it wouldn't be here unless it led somewhere," Mom said.

"And it's not like we've got anywhere better to go," Rachel added.

"Yeah, you're right," Bill admitted. "But the thing that worries me is that we're going into the woods. That means we're going to leave the water's edge where someone on an airboat could see us."

"It also means we won't be seeing any alligators," I reminded him.

We started to follow the old trail. Again it was slow going. The trail was overgrown with brush, and Mom's crutches kept getting caught in vines and branches. And like the day before it had become incredibly hot. Even in the shade of the trees it was like being in a hot dry oven.

"Hey, look at that!" Through the woods ahead, I caught a glimpse of a clearing. In the middle of it was a small, broken-down hut made of logs, branches, and odd planks of wood. Its thatched roof had partially fallen in and it was covered with vines. It was pretty obvious that no one had used it in years.

"The good news is, whoever was here must have come from somewhere," Mom said.

"But, hopefully, not in that rowboat," Rachel quipped.

I think we were all glad to stop and rest. We

helped Mom sit back against a tree, then we peeked inside the hut. Except for the thatching that had fallen in, it was empty.

"Doesn't look like anyone really lived here." Bill sounded disappointed.

"Probably just a stopping-off place," I guessed.

"Hunters and poachers," said Rachel. "I once read about this. There's a whole network of trails, shelters, and boats through the Everglades. The poachers kept them up."

"Poachers?" I said.

"Alligator hides for boots and pocketbooks," Rachel said. "Panther skins. Anything they could kill and sell. They pretty much wiped out the panthers. And now there are alligator farms for people who want the skins."

"They even serve alligator in some restaurants," Bill said.

"That reminds me," I said, suddenly aware that my stomach was growling. "Anyone got anything to eat?"

"I might," Mom answered. She was staring up at a tree.

"See something?" I asked.

She nodded. "Mangos and bananas."

We all looked up. She was right. The bananas looked a little green, but the mangos had a reddish tint that meant they were ripe.

Mom pointed to a small clearing to the left

of the trees. Rising up through the vines and shrubs were tall green plants with thick, bamboolike stalks. "And if I'm not mistaken, that could be sugarcane."

To get the mangos, you just knocked them down with a stick. I can't say they were my favorite fruit, but when you haven't eaten much in twenty-four hours they can taste pretty good. The bananas were harder to get, but by climbing halfway up the tree I managed to knock a bunch down. Like I said, they were still green and hard, but we figured we'd carry them with us. They might come in handy later.

And then there was the sugarcane. It sort of looked like a corn stalk. When you broke the stalk and sucked on it, it tasted really sweet and delicious.

"I bet whoever built that hut planted this stuff," Bill speculated as we stood at the edge of the small plot of sugarcane.

"It probably beat hauling a food supply in," I guessed.

Suddenly we heard a rustling sound. The brush just beyond the sugarcane began to quiver and shake as if something were moving through it.

Bill, Rachel, and I reflexively backed away. There were bears in the Everglades, and panthers, and, of course, alligators.

But what came out of the brush was none of those.

A brown snout poked out.

It . . . was a pig!

And not just one pig, but a whole group of them. Pinkish babies, and a few brown adults, some as large as a big dog, only with shorter legs.

"Pigs!" Bill let out a laugh. "We were afraid of pigs!"

But his laughter was cut short when a boar with curling, pointed white tusks burst out of the brush and grunted angrily at us. The coarse brown hair on the back of its neck stood up and white saliva dripped from its jaws.

Its snout quivered as it faced us and lowered its head like a little bull preparing to charge.

They say that pigs are the smartest hoofed animals. Smarter than horses, deer, and cows. I couldn't say. All I knew was that this boar had a mad look in his eyes. Maybe he thought he had to protect his family. Or maybe he'd had some kind of problem with the person who'd built the cabin.

"Get a stick," I whispered to Bill and Rachel.

Bill frowned. "You don't think—"

He didn't have time to finish the sentence. The boar let out a low grunt, and charged.

15

The boar went for Bill first. Rachel's father never had time to find a stick. That boar was fast. Bill tried to kick it and missed.

"Ahhhh!" he cried out as the boar curled behind him and clamped its teeth around his left leg just above the ankle.

Rachel's father went down. Grunting and snarling, the boar held on to his leg.

I grabbed one of Mom's crutches and swung it down on the pig's back as hard as I could.

Whomp! The stick made a sickening thud when it hit the boar. I was sure I must've broken its back, but the creature hardly seemed to notice.

"Get it off!" Bill cried, trying to shake his leg free. "Get it off!"

Whomp! I hit the boar on the back again.

Crack! Mom's homemade crutch broke in half. The boar squealed and let go of Bill's leg. His left leg just above the ankle was bright red. Drops of blood dripped from the cuff. Bill quickly crawled toward Mom.

Grunting and wheezing, the boar backed away and then stopped and glared at us. You couldn't tell if it was really hurt or just catching its breath before the next charge.

Breathing hard and holding the broken half of Mom's crutch, I stood between the boar and my mom, Bill, and Rachel. The crutch had broken with a long, diagonal crack, leaving my piece with something that resembled a point.

The boar still had that mad look in his eyes. I waited to see what it would do. It seemed weird that this one pig, albeit, a *big* pig, could threaten four people.

But the pig had two things we didn't have: a wild ferociousness and a willingness to use its long sharp teeth.

"Be careful, hon," Mom whispered behind me.

I planned to be more than careful. I planned to do nothing. It was up to the boar. If he attacked, we'd fight. But if he decided to leave, the battle would end right there.

The boar grunted. Ever since it bit Bill, the

saliva around its mouth had turned foamy and pink. I assumed that was Bill's blood. But now drops of redder blood and saliva began to drip from its jaws. Was it hurt and bleeding from inside?

Just go away, I thought. Go back into the brush and get better. We'll forgive you for biting Bill if you'll forgive us for trespassing on your land.

But the boar couldn't read my thoughts.

He lowered his head and grunted. Once again he staggered toward us.

16

It was pitiful. With blood dripping from its mouth, the boar practically dragged itself toward us. We didn't even know what it was fighting about. By now the other pigs and piglets had vanished into the brush.

"Careful," Rachel muttered behind me. "You know what they say about wounded animals."

Yes, I thought, *they're even more dangerous.*

I just wished it would change its mind and go away. I didn't want to kill it. There was no reason.

Leaving a trail of blood, the boar hobbled toward us. I knew then that it wasn't going to quit. It probably didn't know how. Giving up wasn't a choice its mind was capable of making.

"Careful, Justin," Mom warned behind me as I raised the broken half of the homemade crutch.

Whack! I swung it down hard on the boar's head.

The creature went down on its side. Its whole body jerked and shook. A small pool of blood gushed from its mouth and it lay still.

I turned to Bill. He was sitting on the ground with his bleeding leg stretched out. Rachel was kneeling next to him, wrapping the wound with cloth strips she'd torn from her black shirt.

"How is it?" I asked.

"Chewed up pretty good," Bill groaned. "But I don't think anything's broken."

"I think we ought to pack up some mangos and bananas and get out of here before that pig's brothers show up," Mom said.

Rachel turned to her father. "First we have to see if you can walk."

We helped Bill to his feet and watched as he tried to put weight on the wounded leg. Wincing, he took one cautious step and then another.

"It'll be okay," he said. "I can do it."

"Good." Still propped against the tree, Mom held her arms out toward me. "Help me up, Justin. Let's go."

"We have to make you a new crutch," I said.

73

"There's no time for that," Mom said. "I'll make do with one."

There was something urgent in her voice that sounded different from before.

"What's the rush?" I asked.

Instead of answering, Mom looked at Bill.

"What is it, Sara?" Bill asked.

Mom shook her head. "It's probably nothing."

Bill frowned. "Then tell me."

"Well, it's . . ." Mom hesitated. "It's just the way the boar attacked us. And the foam around it's mouth. I mean, it's probably nothing, but—"

"Rabies?" Bill turned pale.

"I don't know, Bill," Mom said. "I'm just worried."

Bill looked at me, but I didn't know anything about rabies. Instead of answering, I turned to Rachel. She seemed to know so much. Maybe she knew the answer.

"There's no way of knowing, Dad," Rachel answered. "We just have to get out of here as fast as we can."

17

We got back on the trail again. With Mom hobbling along on one crutch and Bill limping on his bad leg, our progress was slow.

Mom was the slowest. I walked with her while Rachel went ahead with her father. Every hundred yards or so, Rachel and Bill would have to stop and wait for us. You could see the strain on Bill's face as he worried about whether he had rabies or not. Like someone who knew he might have a time bomb waiting to go off inside.

"I'm sorry," Mom apologized to him. "I know you want to go faster. I'm going as fast as I can. Why don't you and Rachel go ahead? Don't worry about us. We'll catch up."

"What if the trail ends or we come to a fork?" Rachel asked.

"Just leave us some sign," Mom said. "Break twigs or whatever. So we'll know which way to go."

Bill nodded grimly. "Thanks, Sara. I appreciate that."

Rachel and Bill started down the trail again and soon disappeared. I stayed behind with Mom, walking slowly.

"You were very brave before," Mom said as she struggled along on her one crutch.

"Wasn't like I had a lot of choice," I answered with a shrug.

"Still, you saw what that boar did to Bill," said Mom. "You could have been hurt."

"I know," I answered.

"And what do you think of Rachel?"

"Jeez, Mom, I don't know," I said. "I mean, a lot's been going on. It's not like I've had time to think about her."

"I think you have," Mom said.

"I can't believe you want to talk about this now," I said. "I mean, we've crashed in the Everglades. You've got a broken ankle. We don't even know if this stupid trail leads anywhere. People got lost and die out here, Mom. How can you possibly care what I think of Rachel?"

"Humor me," Mom said.

"Why?" I asked, swatting some mosquitoes out of my face.

"Because we're in a lot of trouble and there's very little we can do about it," Mom said. "Don't you find that talking helps ease the tension?"

"I don't know," I said. "I guess."

"So?"

"So?" I repeated.

"She's not what you expected, is she?" Mom said.

"I can't believe we're talking about this," I grumbled.

"I thought I just explained why," Mom said.

"Okay, okay," I said. "If you want to talk so much, let's talk about Bill."

I was hoping Mom would shy away from that and end the conversation. But instead, she accepted my dare.

"Okay," she said.

"So what do you think of him?" I asked.

"I think the more relevant question is what *you* think of him," Mom replied.

"You keep turning everything around and putting it on me," I complained.

"Well, I already know how I feel about Bill," Mom said. "I think once you get past the bluster, he's a good person underneath. He makes mistakes, but we all do."

"It's his fault this happened," I said.

"Let's not get into that again," Mom said. "I could have said no."

"Why didn't you?" I asked.

"Because I didn't want to disappoint him," Mom admitted. "And I really didn't think there'd be a problem. I mean, you have to admit that it was a whole series of unlikely events. You couldn't really expect all those things to go wrong at once."

"But that's exactly why you didn't want to go," I argued. "Because you knew you should never fly unless everything is perfect."

"It's over and done now," Mom said. "Believe me, I've learned my lesson. It's not like any of us will ever do anything like this again."

"That's for darn sure," I agreed.

"But Rachel's not what you thought she'd be either," Mom said, bringing the conversation back to where she began.

"Okay, okay, you're right," I admitted. "I mean, she's a lot smarter than I thought she'd be. I guess it's weird. I mean, the thing I don't get is, if she's so smart, why does she dress like such a punker?"

"Why don't you ask her?" Mom said.

"Oh, sure," I scoffed. "That's just what I want to do while we're lost out here in the Everglades."

"Funny," Mom quipped as she hobbled along beside me, "I couldn't think of a better time."

18

About half an hour later, we caught up to Bill and Rachel. Ahead of them, the trail suddenly disappeared into a broad swath of deep brown mud. Bill and Rachel were standing at its edge with their hands on their hips.

"Now what?" Mom asked.

The swath of mud was maybe fifty feet wide. Like twice as wide as a street. A thin layer of water maybe an inch deep rested over it. Several small alligators rested in the deeper puddles. But when they saw us, they waddled away.

Rachel pointed to the other side of the mud where there was an opening in the brush. "You can see where the trail picks up again."

"How will we get across?" asked Mom.

"You got me." Bill shook his head.

"We were just talking about looking for a way around it," said Rachel.

I turned to Mom and Bill. "You guys stay here. Rachel and I will go look."

I figured we'd split up and Rachel would go to the left while I went to the right.

"Go together," Mom said.

I gave her a look. Did she think this was a social opportunity?

She must have read my mind because she said, "It's too dangerous to go alone. If one of you gets hurt or lost, we might never find you."

There was no trail along the edge of the muddy swath. Rachel and I had to fight our way through the brush and vines that were always thickest near water.

Suddenly the brush at my feet rustled and I jumped, fearing another boar attack. But it was only a medium-size alligator, maybe five feet long. Rachel and I watched as it scurried out of the brush and across the mud without sinking.

We followed the edge of the muddy swath for a while, but it just kept going. Finally I stopped and looked at Rachel.

"What do you think?" I asked.

She shook her head. "We could spend a lot of time looking and not finding anything.

Meanwhile, I'm worried about Dad. I think we should go back."

We started back along the mud's edge, following the trail we'd just made.

"How's your dad doing?" I asked.

"He's scared, but he's trying to be brave," Rachel answered. "I mean, can you imagine what it must feel like to think you might have rabies?"

"How much time do you think we have?" I asked.

"I don't know," Rachel answered. "The number ten keeps popping into my head. But I can't remember whether it means you have ten days after a bite to get the vaccination, or that it takes ten days to kill you."

"There's a big difference," I said.

Rachel smirked. "You're telling me."

We were walking single file. I was in front.

"So what do you think?" I asked.

"About what?" Rachel asked back. "Why do you keep asking me that?"

"I don't know," I said. "You just seem like you know a lot."

"A lot for a girl?" she asked sharply.

"No."

"I told you before, it's just common sense," she said.

"In that case I must not know many people with common sense," I quipped.

"Maybe you don't," she said.

"Because I'm a jock, right?"

"Is that what you are?" she asked with a teasing voice.

I looked back over my shoulder at her. "Very funny. But I'm serious."

"You're serious that I was supposed to know you were a jock?" she asked. "How was I supposed to know that?"

"The same way I know you're a punker," I said.

"Oh, so I'm a punker," Rachel said behind me.

"You saying you're not?" I asked.

"No," she said. "I just think it's interesting how you label everyone."

"Not just me," I said. "The world."

"So let me get this straight," Rachel said. "Because of the way I look, I'm supposed to be a punker. But I can't be a punker because of the way I think. So what am I?"

"You tell me," I said.

"No," she shot back. *"You* tell *me."*

"I can't," I said.

"You mean, there's no one in your school who dresses like me but also has the ability to think?" she asked caustically.

"I couldn't tell you," I said.

"Right." Rachel chuckled. "Because you'd never dare be seen talking to any of them. Your friends might think you were contaminated."

"If you're going to make fun of me, just forget it," I said.

"You know what's funny?" Rachel asked behind me. "I always thought it was the jocks who didn't have brains."

"I said forget it!" I grumbled.

19

We got back to Mom and Bill.

"Find anything?" Mom asked.

I shook my head. "The mud just keeps going."

"We have to get across," Bill said anxiously. He still thought he might have rabies.

"We saw a fairly big alligator crawl across the mud back there," I said. "It wasn't having much trouble."

"You're thinking the mud's firm enough to walk across?" Mom asked.

"Or maybe it's not that deep," I said.

Rachel looked around and found a stick. She leaned out over the edge of the mud and jammed it down. The stick went down about a foot. Rachel turned back and gave me an uncertain look. "It doesn't seem that deep. You think it's worth a try?"

"Of course it is!" Bill sputtered.

I gave my mother a look. Would she agree?

"Be careful," she said.

I untied my shoes and pulled off my socks. Then I rolled up my pants to the knee. I took one tentative step into the mud. It felt thick and firm as my foot slid down and came to rest on something rough. Maybe roots. The mud came halfway up my shin.

I took another step. It was the same thing. My foot went down and then stopped.

"How does it feel?" Rachel asked.

"Not bad," I said. "The hardest part is pulling my foot out for the next step."

I demonstrated by trying to pull my foot out of the muck. I had to lean forward and slowly pull up. As my foot came out, the mud made a sucking, slurping noise. As soon as I pulled my foot out, murky water filled the hole I'd left.

It was slow going, but I was making progress. I managed to go ten feet. Then fifteen. With each step the mud got an inch or two deeper. That made it harder to pull my foot out. Soon I was almost twenty feet across the mud and it still only came up as high as my knee.

I was almost to the middle of the muddy area, and it was starting to look like we'd all be able to get across it.

Then I took a step . . . and the bottom fell out.

20

My foot kept going down through the mud.

To the knee.

To midthigh.

To my hip.

The wet mud felt ominously soothing as it rose over my skin.

I quickly twisted around, hoping to step back onto the roots or whatever had stopped me from sinking before. But it was impossible to get any leverage. No matter how much I struggled, I couldn't get my leg out of the mud.

I was going down.

"*Justin!*" Mom screamed.

She, Bill, and Rachel stood at the edge of the mud with panicked looks on their faces.

"I can't get out!" I yelled.

Mom turned to Bill. "Do something!"

I was still sinking. The mud was up to my waist now.

Bill ducked into the brush and came back with a long branch. He stepped a foot or two into the mud and tried to hold it out toward me. I was just able to grab the thinnest twigs at the end of the branch, but when I tried to hold on, they broke off in my fingers.

"It's not long enough!" Bill said.

"Find a longer one!" Mom cried.

Rachel disappeared into the brush. Bill hobbled up and down along the edge of the mud, searching for a longer stick.

Meanwhile, I was still sinking. The mud was just below my ribs. It was the weirdest sensation. I was being swallowed up by the deep, cool, thick brown muck.

"Just hold on, hon." Mom stood at the edge of the mud with a terrified expression on her face. "Just hold on. We're going to help you."

It was bizarre. Maybe because it was happening in slow motion. But it just didn't feel real. It was much more like a dream. Like it couldn't be happening to me. I couldn't be sinking in the mud. It had to be happening to someone else.

"Just hold on," Mom kept saying.

To what? I wanted to ask, but I didn't. I

knew she was doing the best she could. Even if all she could do was stand there and talk.

It was up to my armpits now. Only my head, shoulders and forearms were out of the mud. As I slowly slid lower, I kept imagining my feet hitting something firm that would stop my descent. But there was nothing. Just the petrifying sensation of endlessness, as if this muddy pit went down forever.

Bill stumbled out of the brush with another branch, but it was clearly too short.

"Do something!" Mom cried at Bill.

"There's nothing . . . nothing I can do," Bill gasped helplessly.

They stood there. I was just twenty feet away. But in that mud, it might just as well have been twenty thousand miles away.

Suddenly Rachel came through the brush carrying a big armload of reeds and sticks and branches. She paused for a second at the edge of the mud to catch her breath. Then she started toward me with a look of grim determination etched on her face.

"What are you doing?" Bill gasped behind her.

Rachel looked back. "I'm going to try to save him."

"But—" Bill began.

It was too late. Rachel was plodding toward me, in what looked like slow motion.

"Hurry!" I grunted. The mud was up to my chin.

It was really difficult for her to pull her feet out of the muck to step forward. "Just hold on," she said.

"To what?" I asked.

Rachel rolled her eyes. When she was about five feet from me, she threw the reeds and brush down on the mud between us.

Then she lay down on them and started to crawl toward me.

"What are you doing?" Bill yelled behind her.

Rachel didn't answer. Her face was only a few feet from mine, and in her eyes was this amazing determination. She reached forward and grabbed my hands with hers.

"Okay, Justin," she said. "Pull and wiggle."

"I'll pull you in with me," I gasped.

"No." Rachel looked back at her dad. "Dad, grab my legs!"

Bill started into the muck. Rachel turned to me again. The mud was up to my lower lip. I was craning my neck to keep my head from going under.

"Come on, Justin." She squeezed my hands tightly. "Wiggle and pull!"

I pulled. I wiggled. I didn't feel myself getting anywhere, but at least I wasn't sinking.

So I pulled and wiggled some more. Rachel's grip on my hands was tight. Bill had Rachel by the ankles and was pulling her. And she was pulling me. It was like a human tug of war against the mud. And it was all happening in an excruciatingly slow rate. But now I saw what she wanted to do. I wasn't going to be able to climb up and out of the muck, but I was slowly tilting toward her. And soon, hopefully, I would be on an angle where I could slide out.

Now I wiggled a different way. Not trying to climb up or step out of the mud, but turning my body sideways in the muck as if to slice through it. Meanwhile I kept my hands locked in Rachel's, and Bill kept pulling her legs.

I was starting to slide out. First my shoulders. Then my arms. It was working!

Rachel and I locked eyes again.

"Thanks," I said.

"Don't thank me yet," she grunted as she stretched. "I just better be two inches taller when this is over."

21

It was over when I was able to crawl on my stomach, out of the muck and onto the mat of brush and reeds that Rachel had thrown down on the mud.

With Rachel in the lead, I stepped wearily back to the edge. I was covered from chin to toe with brown guck. My clothes were saturated with it. Of course, Mom had to hug me and sob for a little while. Then she had to hug Rachel and thank her over and over again.

I couldn't blame Mom for getting emotional. The whole thing had been pretty darn scary.

"So now what?" Bill asked. It was understandable if he seemed a little impatient. Considering the fact that he might be coming down with rabies, you couldn't blame him.

"We cross the mud," Rachel answered.

Mom frowned. "How?"

"The same way Justin and I just did it," Rachel said. "We crawl across on our stomachs."

Her dad and my mom gave her looks of disbelief.

"She's right," I said. "I saw the alligators do it. I got into trouble because I tried to step on the stuff and it couldn't support my weight. But if you crawl across it with your weight spread out over the surface, it could work."

Bill shook his head and patted his belly. "Maybe with your weight spread out, but not with mine."

Rachel rested her chin on her fists and thought for a moment. "Okay, then we'll go back to that old hut and use the boards as a sort of bridge. We'll lay them over the mud and then slide across."

Bill still looked doubtful.

"Come on, Dad," Rachel practically pleaded. "It may be our only chance. It may be *your* only chance."

Bill finally agreed. We left Mom and hurried back to the hut. It was so flimsy that it was easy to pull apart. It was more than an hour and a half before we'd dragged a bunch of boards back to the muddy edge.

"Once we're on the mud, I get the feeling that the important thing is to keep moving," Rachel said. "Don't stop to smell the flowers."

"Do you think you can do it?" I asked Mom.

"I don't remember anyone giving me any other option," Mom replied with a grim look.

22

It worked. By crawling on our stomachs and sliding on the slats of wood, we were able to get all the way across the mud to the other side. Rachel was right. You had to keep moving, but the mud was just firm enough that you could dig your hands into it and pull yourself along.

Once again we followed the trail. Since it seemed to have ended back where we'd found that rotted rowboat, we clung to the hope that it would lead back to a civilized beginning. But our progress was slow and it soon became clear that before we would find the end of the trail, night would find us for a second time.

As the sun started to drop, we came to a spot

under a large old tree where the moss was soft. We were all hungry and thirsty. While Mom and Bill worked on peeling some mangos, Rachel and I went to find some water.

Once again, as we fought through the brush and vines, the mosquitoes were out in humming clouds.

"I'm not sure I can stand another night with these mosquitoes," Rachel groaned as she tried to swat them away with her hands.

"I think it's better if you just give up and let them bite," I said.

"You serious?" she asked.

"It's weird, but after a while they don't seem to bother you as much," I said. "I mean, they still bother you, but it just doesn't seem to bug you as much."

Rachel gave me a crooked smile. "I think I know what you mean."

We worked our way through the underbrush. "So how's your dad doing?" I asked.

"I think he's scared," said Rachel. "Wouldn't you be?"

"Definitely," I said.

Soon we came to the edge of a swamp. I dipped the water pump in it and started to pump. Of course, close to the swamp, the mosquitoes were even worse. But I noticed that Rachel was no longer trying to slap them away.

"Give up?" I asked.

"I think you're right," she said. "If you just try to ignore them, it's better."

"Kind of like one big bite instead of a bunch of little ones," I surmised.

Rachel gave me a crooked smile. "Sure, Justin, if you say so."

As I said before, the pump worked slowly. Rachel and I kneeled by the edge of the swamp.

"You know," I said, mostly to break the silence, "there's something I've been meaning to ask you."

"Does it have to do with punkers and jocks?" Rachel asked.

"No," I said. "I just couldn't help noticing back when you and your dad got to the airport, you didn't want to get out of the car."

"And you want to know why?" Rachel guessed.

"Well, I was wondering," I admitted.

"So why do *you* think I didn't want to get out of the car?" she asked.

I told her how at first I'd wondered if it had something to with a Discman, but then I thought maybe she was afraid of flying in small planes.

"Well, I definitely don't like small planes," Rachel said, "but that wasn't the reason."

"You going to leave me in suspense?" I asked.

"I just didn't want to meet you," Rachel said.

I looked up, surprised.

"Don't look so shocked," Rachel said. "Did you want to meet me?"

I shook my head, then felt my face turn red with embarrassment.

Rachel smiled. "I wouldn't blush if I were you. The mosquitoes think you're advertising."

"Well, I just want you to know it was nothing personal," I said.

"I know. It's just a huge headache," Rachel said. "I mean, new people in your life. Your dad dating someone new. And the possibility of them getting married and moving into a new place. And don't take this personally, Justin, but the idea of suddenly having some *jock* for a stepbrother . . ."

I couldn't help grinning. "Yeah, that's just what I was thinking. I mean, having some *punker* for a stepsister."

"Right." Rachel smiled back. "Who needs it?"

23

When we'd filtered enough water we headed back to Mom and Bill. The four of us sat in the small clearing with our backs against tree trunks. We were all tired and dirty and hot. Thanks to the water purifier and the mangos and bananas, we were able to eat and drink just enough to keep the really painful hunger and thirst at bay.

But nothing would keep the mosquitoes away.

"It would be great if we could start a fire," I said. "At least the smoke would help keep the bugs away."

But we had no matches left, and none of us had any experience with rubbing sticks together.

Once again we prepared for the evening mosquito attack by covering ourselves with mud.

"If we get out of this," Rachel moaned, "I never want to see another drop of mud for as long as I live."

Despite the buzzing in our ears and the unavoidable bites, it was a lot easier to fall asleep that night. We were all exhausted. . . .

Crack!

I sat up with a jolt. It sounded like a bomb had gone off. It was dark and a slight breeze rustled the tops of the trees. I knew I'd slept, but I had no idea for how long. The air felt funny. The bang had been so loud that my ears were still ringing. The weird thing was, everything was still. All the peeps and chirps had stopped.

"What was that?" Bill asked, a slight edge of fear in his voice.

"Don't know," I answered. But I could smell something different in the air. Still groggy and half asleep, I didn't quite understand what it was.

But the answer came quickly.

A blinding explosion of light filled the sky above us.

"Lightning," Mom said.

"But it's not raining," said Bill.

"Heat lightning," said Rachel.

Now I knew what the smell was. "Smoke," I said.

"Fire," Mom realized.

We heard desperate squawks and rapid flapping sounds in the dark sky above us as an invisible flock of birds flew overhead.

The smoke was being carried by the wind. And it seemed to be getting thicker and heavier.

I rose unsteadily to my feet. "I hate to say this, but I think it's coming our way."

24

Another bolt of lightning lit up the sky. For a moment the woods around us appeared as bright as if it were midday. And in that brief moment we could actually see the haze of smoke drifting through the branches and Spanish moss.

"I think it's time to go, guys," I said nervously.

We started down the trail, sometimes feeling our way in the dark. Other times a burst of lightning made it even brighter than daylight. But the smoke coming from behind us was growing thicker.

"We have to go faster," Bill grunted, even though he was limping on his bad leg.

"I can't," Mom groaned as she struggled

along on her one crutch. "I'm sorry. I don't mean to slow everyone down."

"It's not your fault," I said. "But we have to do something."

"Help her," Rachel suggested.

The next thing I knew, Bill and I were practically carrying Mom. Rachel was ahead of us. In the smoky darkness between bursts of lightning she had to slow down and sometimes even stop. I wondered if anyone was thinking what I was thinking—that we were running with no destination in mind.

And we couldn't run forever.

At one point Rachel stopped in the dark. I can't say Bill or I minded. We needed to catch our breaths, even though each breath felt like it was half smoke.

"What's that?" she hissed.

"What's what?" I gasped.

"Listen," Rachel whispered.

I held my breath for a moment and listened. At first all I could hear was the pounding of my heart and my lungs panting for breath. Then from the distance came the faintest roar, like the sound of traffic on a faraway highway.

"A highway?" I asked, puzzled.

"No," Rachel replied grimly. "The fire."

We turned and looked behind us. Through the branches of the trees we could see a reddish glow against the cloudy sky. It was the kind of glow you saw when you got close to a big city and the lights of the city brightened the air above it.

Only, there was no city out here in the Everglades.

The glow was caused by the fire.

The smoke was thicker now. The breeze was blowing in the same direction as the trail we were following. Once again it seemed to imply that the fire was coming toward us. We helped Mom up and started to move. Only now the smoke was thick enough to make it more difficult. It burned our eyes and made us cough.

A deer crashed through the brush. I'm not sure it even saw us. The smoke was as thick as a heavy mist. Maybe it was my imagination, but it seemed as if I could feel heat behind me. The gray ash floating down around us definitely wasn't from my imagination. And neither were the small red-hot embers that were blowing over us and falling here and there.

Suddenly Rachel stopped and pointed ahead. Through the brush we could see the glow of a small fire ahead of us.

"How the . . . ?" Bill wondered out loud.

"The wind," I said. "It's been blowing sparks over us. They land in the dry brush and catch."

"What do we do?" Mom asked.

I looked behind us. The real fire, the *big* fire, was still back there, lighting the sky more brightly now, getting closer all the time.

"We have to keep going," I said.

"But there's fire ahead of us," Bill said.

"I know," I said. "But we'll just have to go around it."

25

The fire ahead of us was small and contained only a few shrubs. It wasn't that hard to get around it. But overhead the hot scalding wind was still blowing and now it was filled with glowing red sparks and even small burning twigs. They fell around us like flakes of red-hot snow. Some of them even fell on us. Instead of being bitten by mosquitoes, we were being stung by tiny hot embers.

The big fire behind us was catching up. We could feel it at our backs and hear the growing roar of the inferno. More fires were springing up around us. It was hard enough to struggle through the brush and trees without having to detour these blazing obstacles. And now it wasn't just the dry brush that was burning. Here and there a whole tree was on fire.

It was getting harder and harder to breathe. It wasn't just the heat and smoke. There were pockets of strange air—clouds of clear, hot gases you'd breathe without getting any oxygen at all and spots where it almost felt as if the fires around us had sucked up all the oxygen the air could provide.

Rachel led the way and Bill and I followed with Mom. Creatures crashed through the brush just out of sight. It was getting harder and harder to get through the forest. More and more fires were springing up. There seemed to be less and less air to breathe. We were all gasping and struggling. Instead of skirting the fires by yards, we were now lucky to get past them with just a few feet to spare.

Creak! Just as we were helping Mom past a particularly nasty fire I heard the sound of wood snapping. Twisting around, I saw a tree trunk falling toward us. It was about as round as a telephone pole, and if I didn't do something quick, it was going to come down right on Bill, Mom, and me.

I had just enough time to give Mom a push.

"Uhhhh!" With a grunt she fell onto Bill, knocking him out of the way.

I dove.

Thump! The tree trunk came down right in the middle of our little group.

For a moment I thought it had missed everyone.

Then I heard Rachel's anguished cry.

26

"It's burning me!" The tree trunk had fallen across Rachel's legs. The trunk was charred, blackened, and smoldering. It wasn't actually burning, but it was hot enough to burn right through her pants.

Rachel began to writhe and squirm and dig her hands into the ground in pain, struggling to get out from under it.

"Rachel!" Bill hurried over to her. He put his arms around the tree trunk and strained to lift it.

It hardly budged.

"She's pinned!" He cried and backed away, staring at his scorched, blackened arms. "It's too heavy!"

The roar of the big fire behind us was louder

now. Ashes and red-hot embers were falling around us like heavy snow.

Rachel was crying in pain.

"What'll we do?" Mom asked.

"I don't know." Her father looked around desperately. The big fire was roaring up behind us. Smaller fires from windblown embers were flaring up all around us.

"We can't stay," Mom said.

"We can't leave her," Bill shouted.

Bill turned to me. "Let's try the log again."

This time Bill and I wrapped our arms around the smoldering log. Even Mom, with her two-day-old broken ankle tried to help lift it. My arms stung as the log burned through my shirt.

"One! Two! Three! Lift!"

I yanked up as hard as I could. I could feel the log lift a little, but it still wasn't high enough for Rachel to get her legs out.

By then the tree trunk was burning my arms. I had to let go.

"It's no use," I gasped. "It's burning us and it's too heavy."

"Help me, please!" Rachel cried. "It hurts!"

The heat was growing unbearable. The burning roar approaching from behind us sounded like a jet engine. You'd take a breath and feel like you'd gotten nothing but pure heat in your lungs.

I dropped to my knees and got my face next to Rachel's.

"There's got to be a way to move this log!" I shouted at her. "Remember leverage? Fulcrums? What?"

Rachel's eyes widened. "Poles," she groaned. "Pry it off."

Poles . . . The only pole around was Mom's last crutch. I grabbed it and jammed it under the log near Rachel's legs. Then I pressed my shoulder against it and pushed as hard as I could.

"It moved!" I yelled.

Bill quickly found a branch. It still had twigs and smaller branches sticking off it, but there wasn't time to worry about that. He jammed it into the ground next to mine and leaned into it.

The log began to move!

"Come on!" I shouted.

Bill and I strained against the poles. Even Mom helped. Meanwhile, we could feel the heat of the main fire scalding our backs. You couldn't turn to look back at it now. It was too hot for that. The roar was growing louder. An unstoppable inferno was marching up behind us.

The log rose just enough for Rachel to squirm

out from under it. She staggered to her feet and into Bill's arms. You could see that the log had burned through the backs of her black jeans and charred the skin on her legs.

"Come on!" I yelled.

Bill and I grabbed my mom and we started down the trail again. Rachel limped ahead.

Meanwhile, the trail was changing. It was something about the trees. They seemed to have taller, darker, thicker trunks. The ground was starting to become soft and spongy.

Crash! Suddenly a large burning branch smashed to the ground just ahead of us. For a moment it didn't make sense. Where had the branch come from? It was far too big to have been carried by the wind.

We stopped and looked up.

Through the billowing smoke and sparks we could see a new terror. The tops of the very trees we were running through were on fire!

27

In amazement, we stared up at a burning sky!

At the same time the world around us was going from black of night to gray as early morning approached.

Crash! Another burning branch fell into the brush beside the trail. Almost instantly, the brush burst into flames.

We had to move again. Rachel staggered ahead on her scorched legs. Bill and I struggled behind with Mom. We got out from under the burning trees and plunged ahead.

The ground was getting spongier. The trees around us were bigger. The air was feeling just a little bit cooler. The roar of the flames wasn't so loud in our ears. Was it possible that we'd outrun the fire?

Without a word, we all seemed to agree to stop, catch our breaths, and look back. We helped Mom sit. I bent over and pressed my hands against my knees. You never saw four more raggedy, desperate-looking, exhausted people. Everyone's hair was wild and disheveled. Our faces were streaked with mud and soot. Our clothes were torn and filthy. Three days in the Everglades and I felt as if we'd become basket cases.

"What happened . . . to the fire?" Rachel asked between gasps for breath.

We looked back. The fire was an orange and yellow glow just visible through the thick, dark tree trunks. Clouds of black smoke boiled up above it. It was just around dawn now, and it seemed as if the winds had died down.

"It's still coming," Bill panted. "Only slower."

He was right. Here beneath these bigger, denser trees there was less dry brush for the flames to race through. Instead, the fire had to jump from treetop to treetop. Meanwhile, it inched down the tree trunks, gradually engulfing them. In the roar of the fire we could hear crashing now—the thunder of the great trees as they fell.

"We have to keep going," I said.

"How much farther?" Mom asked wearily.

It was clear she was exhausted. We were all exhausted.

"Not far," Rachel suddenly answered.

I looked up. "How do you know?"

Rachel waved her arm around. "Cypress trees." She pressed her hand against the spongy earth. "This is probably a swamp in the rainy season. I think we're going to come to water soon."

"I hope you're right." Mom started to push herself up. "Because I don't know how much longer I can go."

28

Bill and I helped Mom up. Once again we started out. The world around us was growing brighter as the sun came up. And with the sun came the wind again. We could feel it blow through the trunks of the cypress trees, blowing the hot smoky air against our backs.

The cypress grove ended suddenly. From the shadows of the great trees, we stepped into what appeared to be a vast field of tall reeds. Squinting and blinking in the sudden sunlight, we followed the trail.

"Still think we're getting closer to water?" I asked Rachel.

"Definitely, yes." As she limped along she pointed at the reeds. "Cattails."

A gust of hot wind blew up above us, and the

sun suddenly vanished behind a thick cloud of smoke. Behind us, the tops of the cypress trees at the edge of the reeds were burning.

"Once the fire gets down into the reeds it's going to come fast again!" Rachel predicted.

That wasn't good news. So far we'd been able to outrun the blaze. But we were weary and exhausted now. My legs felt rubbery and weak. I didn't know how much longer I could keep moving and supporting Mom.

Around us the smoke changed. The smell changed and it seemed to grow lighter. The heat changed, too. I must have become an expert at fires because without looking back I pretty much knew what those changes meant. The fire had leapt down from the cypress trees. It was in the reeds behind us now.

29

The fire swept across the dried reeds in a rolling wave of orange and yellow, throwing off whitish clouds of smoke. And it was moving fast—as if it had a hunger nothing in its way could satisfy.

We kept running, still not knowing what we were running to. Only knowing what we were running from.

And then, like a miracle, I caught a glimpse of something blue ahead of us down the trail through the reeds.

"You see that?" I gasped as I supported Mom.

"Water," Bill grunted with a nod.

We hurried onward and soon reached the edge of the reeds. It really was a miracle. Before us spread a vast blue body of water. Not a swamp or a marsh, but something more like a lake. Across it on the other side was land. Green trees and shrubs . . . and no fire.

And best of all, nestled right there at the water's edge, was a small white rowboat with oars.

"Let's go!" Bill cried, splashing into the water.

The rowboat was tiny. I could see that it was made for two people. But we didn't have time to worry about that now. We got Mom into the bow, then we helped Rachel in.

But it was clear that there was barely room for one more person.

Bill and I stood knee-deep in the water on opposite sides of the rowboat.

"Get in, Justin," he said.

"What'll you do?" I asked.

"I'll hold on to the side and swim along with you," he said.

I shook my head. *"You* get in."

"No, you," Bill insisted.

"Don't argue with me." I couldn't help smiling. "I'm a long-distance swimmer."

That settled it. Bill clambered into the rowboat and sat down on the seat in the middle. He slid the oars into the oarlocks and nodded at me.

I gave the rowboat a good push and then followed it out into the lake. I have to admit that even though I was exhausted, the cool water felt great. I swam a few strokes and then reached up and grabbed the back of the boat. I was so tired, all I could do was hold on and let the boat pull me as Bill rowed.

Then I felt a hand go over mine, as if to make sure I didn't let go.

I looked up.

Rachel was looking down at me with a smile on her face.

30

You might think that now that we had escaped the fire we'd all be happy and chattering away about our good fortune. But no one said a word. Maybe we were all too tired. Maybe we were all too busy looking at what we'd just left behind. The land behind us was almost completely obscured by huge billowing columns of smoke—black smoke, whitish smoke, and a dozen shades of gray.

I held on to the boat with one hand. Bill rowed, pulling me through the water. The cool water was incredibly refreshing and soothing. Feeling it flow over my weary arms and legs almost made me sleepy. It was a good thing Rachel had her hand over mine. The temptation to close my eyes and go to sleep was very strong.

"Oh, my gosh!" Mom's alarmed cry snapped me out of my semi-dreamlike state. She was pointing at something behind the rowboat.

Coming through the water toward us were two round green nostrils . . .

Two round lumps of eyes . . .

A broad green back ridged with pointed scales.

A huge tail swept back and forth, propelling the beast far faster than Bill could row.

It was the biggest alligator I'd ever seen.

31

"*G*et in!" Rachel was leaning over the back of the rowboat, reaching out for me.

I grabbed her hands and started to pull myself up.

"Ahh!" Mom let out a cry as the little boat tipped precariously. Water splashed and for a second I thought the boat was going to roll over and sink. In that instant the choice became clear. If I kept trying to get in, there was a good chance I'd dump everyone into the water.

I turned back to see where the gator was. Just at that second he disappeared under the surface. The rowboat shook as Bill tried to wrench an oar out of the oarlock.

There was nothing left on the surface except a swirl.

Where . . . ?

I knew the answer. Gators grab their prey from underneath and try to pull them down. Drowning is one of their preferred methods of killing.

Treading water above the gator, I was literally a floating duck.

It may have sounded insane, but my only chance was to dive down and meet the beast below.

32

I dove. Luckily, the water of the lake was pretty clear, unlike the swampy murk we'd been in before. Six feet beneath me, a large, whitish blur was headed for my legs. It was the gator's mouth, open.

I managed to kick out of the way, but the gator wheeled around in a flash. These creatures may have had trouble changing direction on land, but they sure didn't have that problem in the water.

But I had a problem. I was running out of breath. It was weird. I'd once had a friend time me and I'd managed to hold my breath in a dead man's float for almost a minute and a half. Here I was underwater for less than ten seconds and already my lungs began to hurt.

The gator was coming for my legs again. In racing we did flip turns against the walls. Not knowing what else to do, I did a flip now.

Once again, the alligator missed.

But now my lungs were burning.

I had to get a breath.

I swung my head up and out of the water and managed to catch a breath. But with my head out of the water I couldn't see what was happening below.

Then something closed around my ankle . . .

And I felt myself being yanked down.

33

I was underwater. It would have been easy to exhale, panic, and drown. Somehow I managed to hold on to my breath. Below me, the gator writhed back and forth, jerking me this way and that. He had my ankle in his jaws, but it wasn't like he was trying to bite hard. He was just holding on and pulling me down. He wanted me to drown. He wanted the water to do the dirty work.

I held my breath and tried to relax. I knew I couldn't fight this monster on its home turf. My only chance was to play possum and wait.

It worked. The instant I felt him loosen his grip on my ankle, I jerked it out of his mouth and kicked as hard as I could toward the surface. I knew he'd come after me, but first I had to get another breath.

I must've caught him by surprise because I made it to the surface and actually had time to exhale and take a new breath. When I ducked my face down into the water again, he was right below me, the wide white jaws open again, coming up for another grab.

Just as his jaws snapped shut, I did another roll. A weird moment followed as we passed each other in the water. His momentum was sending him up while mine was sending me down.

Then I remembered what Rachel had said when we were in the marsh: *The muscles that open their jaws are much weaker than the muscles that close them. Your best chance is getting an arm around his mouth and holding it closed.*

What did I have to lose?

34

I reached out and got my arm around his mouth and hugged it tight to my body.

Boy, he didn't like that.

Kicking and flailing like a bucking bronco, he tried everything he could to get me to let go.

Meanwhile, I held my breath and held on for dear life.

Still fighting, he twisted his head left and right and dug at my body with his claws. It took all my strength to hold my breath and hold on.

But I was running out of air.

The gator thrashed under the water. My lungs started to burn. I don't know why I hung on. I just couldn't think of anything else to do.

Finally my lungs felt like they were going to

explode. I had to get air. I let go of the gator's snout and shot up to the surface. Air never tasted so good, but it didn't seem to help.

It didn't give me the energy I needed to keep fighting.

I guess I was just too tired.

I was beyond tired. I couldn't move. I could hardly gather the energy to focus, and besides, my vision was blurred from the water. I knew I was close to the boat, but I couldn't reach it. I could hear Rachel screaming at me, reaching out toward me.

But there was nothing I could do.

Just then a shadow rose up behind Rachel in the boat.

Dad?

My vision was blurred and I was half-conscious from lack of air. It couldn't be him, but . . . then who?

He had something long and narrow in his hand.

There was a sudden movement. The long narrow thing plunged straight down into the water beside me. The water suddenly became turbulent. I knew it must have been the gator thrashing, but I didn't know why.

Then, just as suddenly as the water became turbulent, it grew calm. A hand grabbed the collar of my shirt. Once again I felt the sensation of being towed slowly through the water.

I looked up. At first I only saw blue sky.

Then Rachel's blurry face appeared above me.

"You okay?" she asked.

"I think so."

"Still got all your arms and legs?"

My ankle throbbed painfully where the gator had gotten it. But I could still move my foot. "Think so."

Rachel grinned. "Good. Those are the kinds of things jocks like you need."

35

"So what did I tell you?" Bill asked loudly. "Is this great or what?"

It was one week later and the four of us were lounging on the terrace of Palm Resort in Key West. The round orange sun was just moments from setting behind a small island across the harbor.

Bill turned to me. "Bet you never thought you'd make it here, huh, Justin?"

There were a couple of dozen people up on the terrace and every one of them could hear him. Of course, they all knew who we were. Mom's leg was in a cast up to her knee. My ankle was bruised and still painful. Bill had a big bandage on his leg where the boar had bitten him (he'd also gotten rabies shots), and Rachel had bandages on the backs of both legs where the smoldering tree trunk had burned her.

"You're right," I said.

The strangers around us nodded. We might not have known them, but they all knew us from the newspapers and television. We were the amazing survival story of the week. We'd survived a plane crash, quicksand, wild boars, a forest fire, and, of course, the attack of a giant alligator.

Now I knew that the shape that had loomed up behind Rachel in the rowboat was Bill. And that the long straight thing was an oar, which he had plunged down the alligator's throat as it swam up to finish me off.

A woman wearing black slacks and a white shirt came up to us. She was carrying a tray and had three pens in her shirt pocket. "Excuse me, sir," she said to Bill, "but minors aren't allowed up here after sunset."

Bill turned to her with a broad smile. "Do you know who we are, miss?"

"Yes, sir," the woman replied. "You're the people from the plane crash. But it's the rule here."

"Well, I think you could make an exception," Bill blustered.

"I wish we could, sir," the young woman replied firmly, "but if we make it for you we have to make it for everyone."

Rachel and I shared a look and got up.

"Where are you going?" Bill asked.

"We're going to take a walk down to the dock," I said.

"Don't stay out too late," Mom said.

Rachel and I left the Palm Resort and walked past the T-shirt stores and souvenir shops toward the dock. It was a warm balmy night and a lot of people were out. We sat down on the concrete seawall, put our feet over, and watched a sailboat cruise past, turning into a silhouette as the sun disappeared.

"So what do you think?" Rachel asked.

"About what?" I asked back.

"Our parents," she said. "Think they should get together?"

"Sure, why not?" I said with a shrug.

"Think you can put up with my dad?" Rachel asked.

"I don't know," I said. "But at least I know what I'm getting for a stepsister."

We shared a smile.

So, what do *you* think?" I asked.

"I guess a jock for a stepbrother would be okay," Rachel replied.

After that we just looked up at the sky and watched the stars slowly appear. So far, so good.

ABOUT THE AUTHOR

Todd Strasser has written many award-winning novels for young and teenage readers. Among his best-known books are those in the *Help! I'm Trapped In . . .* series. Todd speaks frequently at schools about the craft of writing and conducts writing workshops for young people. He and his wife, children, and Labrador retriever live in a suburb of New York. Todd and his family enjoy boating, hiking, and mountain climbing.

You can learn more about Todd and the *Against the Odds* series at www.toddstrasser.com.

Todd Strasser's
AGAINST THE ODDS ™

Shark Bite
The sailboat is sinking, and Ian just saw the
biggest shark of his life.

Grizzly Attack
They're trapped in the Alaskan wilderness
with no way out.

Buzzard's Feast
Danger in the desert!

Gator Prey
They know the gators are coming for
them...it's only a matter of time.

A MINSTREL® BOOK
Published by Pocket Books

2023

When ___ ___ ___ ___ ___ ___ Rod
Allb___ ___ ___ ___ ___ ___ werful
alie___ ___ ___ ___ ___ ject ___od is
dra___ ___ ___ ___ ___ tch a
dan___ ___ ___ ___ ___ them
all ___

I LE___ ___ $3.99

Sim___
200
Pleas___ ___ cover the
postag___ ___ —no cash
or C.C___ ___ ___ SA: card
numbe___
Name___
Addr___
City ___
VISA___
Signa___ ___ 043-04